Say Hola to Spanish

by Susan Middleton Elya

illustrated by Loretta Lopez

Lee & Low Books Inc. • New York

Text copyright © 1996 by Susan Middleton Elya
Illustrations copyright © 1996 by Loretta Lopez
All rights reserved. No part of this book may be reproduced
by any means without the written permission of the publisher.
LEE & LOW BOOKS Inc., 95 Madison Avenue, New York, NY 10016

Printed in Hong Kong by South China Printing Co. (1988) Ltd.

Book design: Christy Hale
Book production: Our House
Editorial consultant, Spanish language: Daniel Santacruz

The text is set in Benguiat Frisky, La Bamba and Marguerita.
The illustrations are rendered in gouache and colored pencil on watercolor paper.

10 9 8 7 6 5 4 3 2 1
First Edition

Library of Congress Cataloging-in-Publication Data

Elya, Susan Middleton,
Say hola to Spanish/by Susan Middleton Elya;
illustrated by Loretta Lopez.
p. cm.
Summary: Introduces Spanish by defining such common words
as "hola" ("hello"), "perro" ("dog"), and "madre" ("mother").
ISBN: 1-880000-29-6
1. Spanish language—Vocabulary—Juvenile literature.
[1. Spanish language—Vocabulary] I. Lopez, Loretta,
II. Title.
PC4445.E49 1996
468.1—dc20   95-478
CIP
AC

To my husband Robert, and our kids:
Carolyn, Nicholas, and Janine—S.M.E.

To my family: Belia (Mom), Ed Jr., Armida, Gil, Sal,
and especially Ed Sr.—up in the stars . . .
X O X O X—L.L.

Spanish is fun,
so give it a try.

¡Hola!

Hola is hello,

¡Adiós!

adiós is good-bye.

A dog is a **perro**,
a cat is a **gato**.

You drink from a **vaso**

and eat from a **plato**.

A son is an **hijo**,

a mother is a **madre**,

daughter is **hija**,

and father is **padre**.

You play in a **parque**,

you live in a **casa**.

Mamá drinks coffee,
café, from a **taza**.

Your hair is your **pelo**,

your nose is **nariz**.

Your grandmother's **pelo**
is probably **gris**.

You sit on a **silla**,

you eat at a **mesa**.

A perfect surprise is called a **sorpresa**.

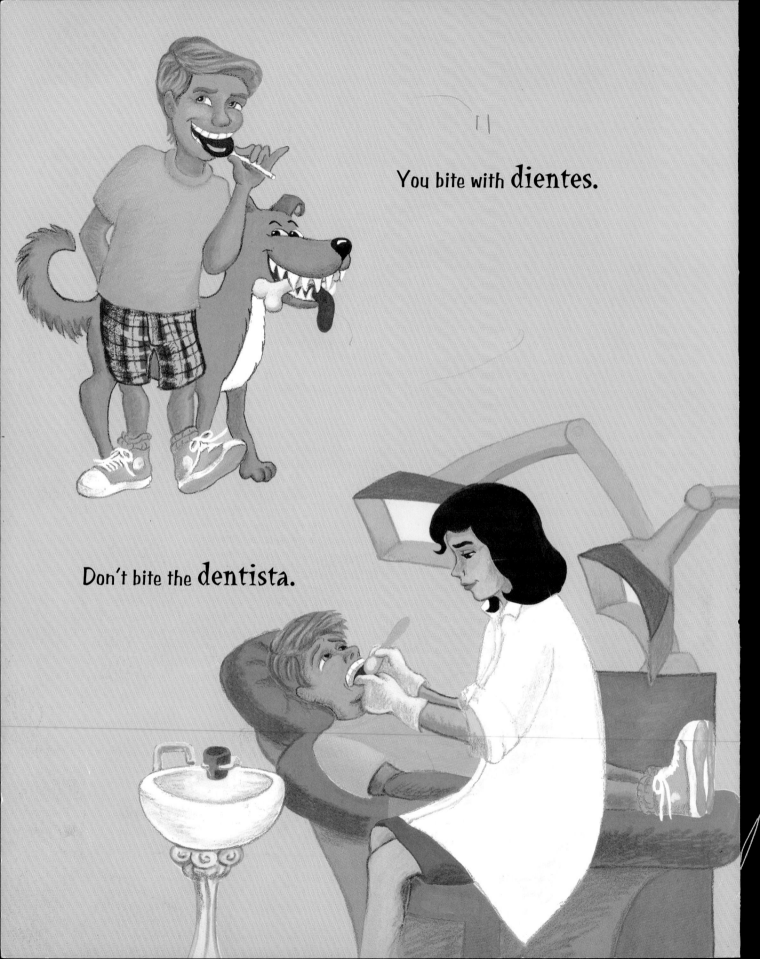

You bite with **dientes.**

Don't bite the **dentista.**

Just wait for your check-up and read a revista.

You study in an escuela
and dance at a fiesta.

Your afternoon nap
is called a siesta.

A boy is a **niño**,

a girl is a **niña**.

He eats a **pera**,
she eats a **piña**.

Besos are kisses.

Smiles are **sonrisas.**

Blusas are blouses and shirts are **camisas.**

Your dad drives a **carro**, same thing as a **coche**.

He drives in the **día** and drives in the **noche**.

A tree is an árbol,

¡Yipe!

a flower is a flor.

Cierra la puerta means shut the door!

Ham is **jamón** and soup is called **sopa**.

You wash with **jabón**

and get dressed in **ropa**.

Wish at a fountain.

Throw coins in the **fuente**.

Deseos come true. It's no accidente!

A man who makes shoes is **un zapatero.**

Zapatos, or shoes, cost lots of **dinero.**

The hat on your head is called a **sombrero**.

A cowboy on horseback is called a **vaquero**.

Caliente is hot.

Cold is called frío.

You fish at a lago and raft down a río.

A secret you'll tell an **amigo** or friend.
Amigos keep **secretos** up to the end.

In English and Spanish a burrito's a **burrito**.

A piñata's a piñata

and a mosquito's a mosquito.

Hola is hello, adiós is good-bye.

Spanish is fun, so give it a try!

Glossary

accidente (ahk-see-DEN-teh): accident
adiós (ah-dee-OCE): good-bye
amigos (ah-MEE-goce): friends
árbol (AHR-bol): tree
besos (BEH-soce): kisses
blusas (BLUE-sahs): blouses
burrito (boo-RREE-toe): burrito
caballo (kah-BYE-yoe): horse
café (kah-FEH): coffee
caliente (kah-lee-EN-teh): hot
camisas (kah-MEE-sahs): shirts
carro (KAH-rroe): car
casa (KAH-sah): house
cierra la puerta (see-EH-rrah la PUER-tah): shut the door
coche (KOE-cheh): car
dentista (den-TEE-stah): dentist
deseos (deh-SEH-oce): wishes
día (DEE-ah): day
dientes (dee-EN-tehs): teeth
dinero (din-EH-roe): money
escuela (ehs-KWEH-lah): school
fiesta (fee-EH-stah): party
flor (FLOOR): flower
frío (FREE-oh): cold
fuente (FWEN-teh): fountain
gato (GAH-toe): cat
gris (GREECE): gray
hija (EE-hah): daughter
hijo (EE-hoe): son
hola (OH-lah): hello
huesos (WEH-soce): bones
jabón (hah-BONE): soap
jamón (hah-MONE): ham
lago (LAH-goe): lake
loro (LOE-roe): parrot
madre (MAH-dreh): mother

manos (MAH-noce): hands
mesa (MEH-sah): table
mosquito (moe-SKEE-toe): mosquito
nariz (nah-REECE): nose
niña (NEEN-yah): girl
niño (NEEN-yoe): boy
noche (NOE-cheh): night
ojos (OH-hoce): eyes
padre (PAH-dreh): father
pan (PAHN): bread
parque (PAR-kay): park
pelo (PEH-loe): hair
pera (PEH-rah): pear
perro (PEH-rroe): dog
el piano (el pee-AH-noe): the piano
piña (PEEN-yah): pineapple
piñata (peen-YAH-tah): piñata
plato (PLAH-toe): plate
quesos (KEH-soce): cheeses
revista (rreh-VEE-stah): magazine
río (RREE-oh): river
ropa (RROE-pah): clothing
secretos (seh-CREH-toce): secrets
siesta (see-EH-stah): nap
silla (SEE-yah): chair
sombrero (sohm-BREH-roe): hat
sonrisas (sone-REE-sahs): smiles
sopa (SOE-pah): soup
sorpresa (sor-PREH-sah): surprise
taza (TAH-sah): cup
toro (TOE-roe): bull
vaca (BAH-kah): cow
vaquero (vah-KEH-roe): cowboy
vaso (VAH-soe): glass
zapatos (sah-PAH-toce): shoes
un zapatero (sah-pah-TEH-roe): a shoemaker